A SECRET HISTORY OF PORT TOWNSEND VOLUME I

The Thing Army Engineers Unearthed at Fort Worden

DYLAN JAMES QUARLES

RAINIER-AUGUSTA

SETTLERS, GHOSTS, AND RURAL WATERWAYS: AN OVERVIEW

DR. D. B. CALDWIN, PROFESSOR OF SOCIAL AND ECONOMIC HISTORY VERMONT UNIVERSITY

Port Townsend Washington is a picturesque Victorian seaport on the Northeastern tip of the Quimper Peninsula, which is itself a protrusion of the larger, more well known Olympic Peninsula. Typically, the town boasts a population of around 11,000, however this number is known to swell and shrink depending on the arrival of tourists and seasonal workers.

The first nonnative settlers arrived in 1851, yet archaeological evidence shows inhabitation by the Klallam tribes, dating back at least another 400 years. Nevertheless, the new arrivals soon took over and began at once the work of capitalizing on natural resources and trade. Thanks to its strategic placement at the mouth of the Puget Sound (a vast inlet of the Pacific Ocean, feeding cities such as Seattle, Tacoma and Olympia), Port Townsend quickly became a bustling port of entry. Vessels from far and wide passed through, trading, transporting, and trafficking in all manner of goods. Innumerable fortunes were made, leading to the construction of a charming brick and stonework downtown corridor, overseen by a host of steepled, asymmetrical Victorian mansions on the hill.

For a time, it seemed that Port Townsend was positioned to become one of America's great cities. Unfortunately, the critical absence of a railway, coupled with the relative shallowness of its bay, prohibited Port Townsend from expanding operations to meet the needs of other, larger cities along the Puget Sound. Like a grape—withering on the vine—Port Townsend dimmed until it was but a husk of its former self. Things fell quiet and the town became frozen in time. The old brick and stonework buildings sprouted webs of ivy, while the mansions on the hill gradually peeled in the briny fog.

Then, in 1896, Congress took action to bolster the security of America's waterways. Funding was allocated for the construction of a military fortification at the mouth of the now vital Puget Sound inlet. Joined by its island neighbors, Whidbey and Marrowstone, Port Townsend was selected as the primary point of the aptly-dubbed Triangle of Fire. Work began immediately and an army of engineers, builders, and enlisted men descended upon the town. For the next five years a sprawling complex of barracks, administrative buildings, officers houses, parade grounds, gun batteries, fortifications, bunkers, and tunnels were constructed along the northern shoreline of the Quimper Peninsula. Dug deep into the domed hill above the beachhead, these newly minted installations were collectively christened, Fort Worden. Home to the Headquarters for Coastal Defense, Fort Worden remained an active military installation until June of 1953 when it was publicly retired. During all of that time, Fort Worden and Port Townsend lived side-by-side, symbiotically supporting one another through good times and bad.

Now a popular State Park, Fort Worden boasts a museum of coastal artillery, a cafe, a marine science center, and even a community college. Moreover, its many bunkers and batteries can be accessed by walking trails, which criss-cross the entirety of the colloquially known, Artillery Hill. Each year, tens of thousands of holiday visitors flock to Fort Worden to rent rooms in its old Officer's houses, or camp at the beach. Occasionally, rumors emerge about sounds heard, or things glimpsed in the maze-like network of subterranean tunnels beneath the hill. People claim to see strange apparitions, unexplainable figures, or even floating clusters of geometric lights. It is my opinion that these incidents are simply the result of overactive imaginations, fueled by campfire ghost stories. Surely, they hold no basis in reality.

4

THE MAINTENANCE MAN

Rick Concord strolled across the Fort Worden State Park campus, making his way toward the Commons cafe through the chilled and leafy autumnal morning. Clipped to his belt, a large cluster of keys kept the rhythm of his gate. Neither tall nor short, fit nor fat, the 52 year old maintenance man seemed somehow unimpressive when compared with his surroundings.

Hunkered beneath a nebulous dome of clouded skies, a collection of pre-war military buildings and stately officer's houses checkered the tree-lined bluff down to the beach below. There, gray waves crashed against the breakwater of point Wilson, haloing its picture-perfect light house in a spray of frigid sea, and sending mists climbing up the cliff face of nearby Artillery Hill.

A savage cry split the scene, causing Rick to give a start of surprise. He turned, spotting a pair of police officers wrestling a filthy, blood-soaked man into the back of their cruiser. Already in cuffs, the man writhed and screamed, his left ear dangling from the side of his head by a thread of red sinew.

"You can't do this!" He wailed. "I'm from here! It's still happening! It's still happening!"

THE UNCERTAIN FUTURE OF
THE PARANORMAL PORT
TOWNSEND PODCAST

The Commons cafe was abuzz with community college students, fueling up before the day's classes began. Rick entered, spotting his friend Lief amongst the throngs.

"Hey guy," said Lief, closing his laptop as Rick approached. "I was just editing this Friday's episode on house 4 East. Your interview was—pretty ok. Did you get a chance to check your hunting cameras yet? Tell me you got something I can put up on the website."

Rick sat down with his coffee and sighed.

"Afraid not."

"What? I thought 4 East was haunted with a shower ghost —you told me. That footage was going to be clutch! Without it, it's just me talking out my ass again."

"4 East *is* haunted," said Rick. "At least ten different groups of guests have seen a man in the shower since I've been here—at least."

"Then what's the deal, Rick?"

Faltering, Rick felt his cheeks begin to burn.

"Easy big guy," grinned Lief. "I'm just giving you a hard time. I mean, that *was* my whole episode, but whatever. Paranormal Port Townsend was a dumb idea for a podcast. I don't even think I have ten subscribers."

He drummed his fingers on the tabletop, adopting an expression Rick had come to recognize as his thinking face.

"Do you have keys to any of those locked doors up on Artillery Hill?"

"What locked doors?"

"Haven't you seen them? Big metal doors with padlocks. They're up where the giant mortars used to be—the big U shaped bunkers dug into the hill."

"Oh those," said Rick. "That's just where we keep old paint cans."

Lief looked crestfallen and put his laptop away.

"Well—I should probably get to class. I'm not loving my economics teacher, but I paid for it so..."

He stood to leave, then hesitated.

"It's just that I heard this weird story the other day. Do you know Boatyard Bill?"

Rick nodded.

"The guy is like a quantum alcoholic," said Lief. "Always somehow simultaneously at every bar in town, but that's not what I wanted to say. No, I ran into him last night buying smokes at PennySaver—"

"You gotta knock that off, kid," Rick interrupted. "Take it from me."

"Yeah ok," said Lief. "Anyway, he was telling the sandwich girl—you know the one with purple hair?"

"I know her."

"He was telling her that Artillery Hill is a vortex."

Knitting his brow, Rick tried to recall if he had ever heard that one before. As a native of Port Townsend, his mind was cluttered with old ghost stories and tales of strange encounters. The area was a treasure trove of paranormal lore, and Fort Worden was its Hope Diamond.

"Does Bill mean a vortex like the Oregon vortex—the one out in Gold Hill?"

"Not exactly," said Lief. "More like a supernatural vortex —at least that's the way he described it. He said that's why Port Townsend has so many ghosts and haunted houses. Apparently, there's, like, an epicenter somewhere on Artillery Hill and it kind of holds all of the ghosts in orbit."

As had always been his nature, Rick found himself unable to dismiss the idea out-of-hand.

"Where did Bill say the epicenter to this vortex was?"

Sitting back down, Lief adopted a confidential air.

"In the tunnels—hence my question about those locked doors."

Rick imagined the untold miles of subterranean tunnels burrowed throughout Artillery Hill by Army engineers in the early 1900's.

A memory surfaced, unearthed by new information.

"There is a door," he muttered absently. "A locked door in the tunnels—I've seen it."

"There is? Not just another door with old paint cans inside?"

"I—" faltered Rick. "I don't know what's behind it. I've never opened it."

"Do you have the keys?"

"Of course I do," he answered. "I work maintenance."

"Then we have to go!" Lief practically shouted.

Laughing nervously, he glanced around the busy cafe and lowered his voice.

"For the show I mean—we could do an on-location episode! I mean, it would be something, right? Better than nothing. Besides, I know you don't have a life outside of this place. We'll go tonight after I get out of class."

THE GIANT'S TOOTH

Nearing the end of its westward arc, the sun sank behind the ridge of Artillery Hill. One by one, the many street lamps and porch lights of Fort Worden flicked on, yet they could do little to forestall the transformation that nightly turned the old campus into a haunted graveyard of otherworldly shapes.

"Sorry I'm late!" Said Lief, climbing into Rick's car. "How was your day?"

Rick blinked, not used to people asking him such questions.

"Fine," he shrugged. "Trouble with the boiler in 225—found a bunch of drowned rats in the pump."

"Cool," said Lief with a shudder. "And what about our little expedition? Do we have everything we need for tonight?"

Rick nodded toward the backseat.

"Got a duffle sack with flashlights, game cameras, batteries—a few tools too."

"Then let's roll, big Rick!"

The pair drove to a large metal gate at the base of

Artillery Hill, Lief narrating their progress into his digital recorder. Parking beneath a twisted madrone, Rick grabbed the duffel and took out two flashlights.

"There are no street lamps or flood lights up there. No power. Easy to get turned around—eyes playing tricks on you. Even for me."

The hill loomed large in the failing light, its profile like that of a giant tooth worn flat from eons of grinding bone. Passing the gate, the two wound upwards along an old military road that carved through the windswept coastal forests. Carried by the breeze, disembodied sounds echoed through the trees, hailing from the neighborhoods and surrounding hills. Barking dogs became laughing lunatics. Worn brake pads—the screams of brutalized women. Near the summit, breaks in the tree line gave way to vistas, so sweeping and huge they seemed surreal. The wine-dark waters of the Salish sea churned, fat with monstrous black creatures that slithered up from the kelp forest to ride the outgoing tide. Across the inlet, Whidbey Island smoldered silently, great streamers of hot ash trailing up into the sky as yet another wildfire consumed the inner grasslands.

The two men came to a fork in the road with many crooked tongs. Some, little more than footpaths, wound north along the cliff, while others led to the various bunkers and gun batteries which gave the hill its name. Dug into the earth by long-forgotten workmen, these concrete edifices honeycombed the landscape like the ancient ruins of a lost civilization.

"So where was that locked door you mentioned?" Asked Lief, holding the recorder up to Rick.

"Near the old Harbor Defense Command Post. I was with Ranger Tom and some guys from the recording studio who wanted to use the big cistern. Something about the acoustics."

"And that's where you saw the door? In the cistern?"

"Not there exactly."

"Then where? I don't want a repeat of our shy shower ghost here, Rick."

"It's near the cistern," said Rick defensively. "I'll show you."

They stepped off the main road, embarking on a narrow footpath that wound through a grove of naked madrone trees. Here and there, unmarked bunkers lurked the wooded hollows, some so overgrown that they seemed more ancient than the land itself. The winds kicked up over the straights, lacing the hill with cool fingers of briny fog. Darkness descended and Rick was forced to turn on his flashlight. Diffused by the mists, its beam scanned the wilted rhododendrons that lined the way, until a subtle break made it stop and hold steady.

"Is there a bunker back there?" Said Lief, moving in for a better look. "That shouldn't be there. I mean—it's not on any of the bunker maps they hand out at the Commons."

Rick chuckled softly.

"There are lots of tunnels that didn't make the tourist map, kid. You'd only know this was here if you came in the fall, or winter when all the rhodies die off."

He parted the bushes, fully revealing the entrance to a narrow concrete aperture in the hillside.

"Or, if you were actually from here."

"All right," said Lief. "Calm down. townie."

He raised his flashlight and read the words spray painted above the entrance.

"*Hell*. Sounds promising."

As if in response, the wind caught the corner of the tunnel's mouth and let out a low groan.

"Oh this is too good," laughed Lief. "I've got to get that for the show. Let's put a camera here too—what do you say?"

They set to work, Rick affixing one of his motion acti-vated trail cameras to a tree across the path from the tunnel, while Leif recorded the groaning of the wind. Their tasks complete, they quit the foggy night and ducked through the tunnel's entrance.

CERBERUS

At first, there was little to see, beyond the low ceiling and cramped walls. The tunnel sloped downhill precipitously, sometimes veering into the dangerous. Dead leaves scattered the floor and dangling cobwebs made for sticky progress.

Rick stared ahead into the blackness, while Leif panned his flashlight along the wall, reading from the spray painted messages that had been left by decades of local teenagers.

"Dez Nutz," he said in mock seriousness. "RIP Harambe. Jenny Witwood is a slu—"

An unearthly howl drifted up from the darkness, silencing Lief's voice like a knife across the throat.

Both men froze.

"Do you hear that?"

"The wind again?"

"I don't think so—maybe. I didn't feel any wind. It's coming from the wrong direction anyway, isn't it?"

The howl faded, its lingering echoes filled with lupine intonations.

"We should turn back," said Rick.

"Turn back? Are you nuts? This is exactly what we came here for!"

"But—"

"Listen, man—you turn back if you want. Just give me your keys and I'll handle the rest."

Rick flushed in the darkness, thankful that Lief's light was not pointed at his face.

"Come on," he muttered. "Let's go."

They continued on, the tunnel leveling out, then narrowing. Rainwater had accumulated to form a brackish sludge that undulated with each step. Hearing ill omens whispered in the lapping susurrations, Rick felt the first warning signs of claustrophobia.

The nightmare wound deeper, following a path that mirrored the borings of a parasitic beetle through old timber.

"Look!" Said Lief after a bit. "Look there!"

Rick glanced up, a rusty metal doorway materializing in the glow of their flashlights. Strung with cobwebs, it framed another tunnel which extended forever onwards into the bowels of the hill.

"Is that it?" Said Lief. "Is that the door you saw? Looks pretty unlocked to me."

The howl returned with urgency, seeming to emanate from just beyond the range of their flashlights. Rick put a hand to his chest, wincing.

"Holy Toledo!" Exclaimed Lief. "It's right there!"

He dashed toward the doorway, swiping cobwebs from his path.

"Kid," shouted Rick after him. "This is a bad idea."

The howl reached an unbearable crescendo, morphing into three vaguely different voices. Ignoring the obvious danger it posed him, Lief stepped over the threshold and into the new tunnel.

"You don't know what you're doing," said Rick, feeling dizzy. "You're not from here."

He went to the doorway, stumbling through in an attempt to catch his young friend by the arm and draw him back to safety.

"Please," he wheezed. "We can't be here."

Lief spun in anger, ready to hurl insult and injury. And yet, the second he did so, his face drained entirely of color. Rick felt the shift behind him, the reordering of space to accommodate another presence in the tunnel. The hairs on the back of his neck stood up and the whispering susurrations of the brackish water screamed in terror.

With the force of a bomb, the howl erupted behind him and the door slammed shut. Knocked to the ground, both men lost hold of their flashlights, allowing darkness to descend; bedfellow of insanity.

INFERNO

Hours passed, but how many, neither could say. Pounding on the metal door, beating their fists bloody, they tried in vain to force it open again. At one point, Lief dug into Rick's duffel sack and came back with a hammer.

He attacked the hinges, showering sparks that flared and died like doomed souls.

"It's no use," panted Rick. "We're trapped."

"No," said Lief, grunting with effort. "No fucking way."

He struck at the hinges again, the hammer ringing dully.

"Open—god—damn—you!"

"Kid," said Rick. "It's over. It's not going to open—he won't let it. We have to find another way out."

Succumbing to the reality of their situation, Lief slumped to the floor and hugged his knees. Framed in the circle of Rick's flashlight, propped-up on the ground nearby, his shadow became that of a little boy. Rick watched him dispassionately, then turned his eyes on the tunnel behind them. Something stirred in the inky blackness, accompanied by a faint hiss.

Lief heard it too and looked up, wiping tears from his eyes.

"What—"

"Shhhh," said Rick. "Look."

He retrieved his flashlight and angled its beam down the tunnel. A figure took shape at the edge of illumination, young, slight of build, and wearing the baggy clothing of a skateboarder. The boy raised his hand, holding something metallic and cylindrical. Again, the hissing sound flared, tied to the motion of his arm.

Rick wrinkled his nose, smelling spray paint fumes in the stagnant air.

"Hey!" Shouted Lief, jumping up. "Hey kid!"

The figure turned toward them, continuing to spray the wall with looping strokes of misty paint.

"We're trapped. How'd you get down here?"

"I wouldn't worry about that, bro," answered the spray painter, his voice carrying with unnatural clarity. "Ain't the getting in you gotta worry about. It's the getting *out*."

"What's that supposed to mean?" Demanded Lief. "This isn't a joke!"

He hefted the hammer and stalked forward. Adding one final flourish to his work, the spray painter dropped his can and turned to go.

"Wait!" Cried Lief, breaking into a run. "Wait—don't leave us!"

He crossed before the beam of Rick's flashlight, blotting it out with his spidery shadow as he ran after the man.

"Don't leave us, damn you! Come back!"

Seeing that his friend was not going to stop, Rick collected the duffel sack and joined the pursuit. Slowing only where the spray painter had marked the wall, he allowed himself a beat to read the words.

THROUGH ME YOU PASS INTO ETERNAL
    ~~*PAIN*~~ *DARKNESS.*
BLINDED BY THE LIGHT, ALL REVVED UP
    & NO PLACE TO GO.
I AMONG THE PEOPLE LOST AYE. PASS
    INTO THE CITY OF WOE.
PARADISE BY THE DASHBOARD LIGHTS:
    PRETTY LIGHTS, MINING LIGHTS.
MINE MY MIND, MAN. ETERNAL, &
    ETERNAL
I ENDURE. ABANDON ALL HOPE YE WHO
    ENTER HERE & EAT MY SHORTS.

Thick with dust and cobwebs, the can of spray paint lay on the ground where it had been dropped; as timeless a fixture to the tunnel as the blooms of corrosion which stippled the cracks in the aged concrete.

LOST BEYOND TIME AND SPACE

Without the sky to mark the passage of time, minutes bled into hours, bled into days. Careening through the darkness, the two captives tumbled ever further down the rabbit hole, chasing that which could not be caught. The tunnel branched and split, then branched and split again. New paths converged and diverged, each as fathomless as the last. Doorways appeared at random, portals into empty rooms piled high with the hoarded refuse of giant rats. Damp with mildew and panic, the air grew thick and poisonous. Succumbing to unknown forces, their cellphones drained of battery and died. In order to preserve what little power they had left in the flashlights, they joined themselves together with a length of rope and groped, unseeing, through the vacuum of total darkness. When they reached dead ends, or corridors too flooded to navigate, they turned on the lights and crouched like wretched animals; eating candy bars from the duffel sack and communicating in grunts. They made nests of whatever fetid trash they could find and tried to poach a few hours of sleep. In these restless interludes, Rick would lay awake, listening to Lief muttering half-formed sentences and gibberish into his recorder. Too exhausted to manage his friend's mental decline, he did, however, make a point to steal away the hammer.

It happened on the third day. Or, maybe the fourth. Feeling blindly along a wall, as he so often did, Rick began to become aware of a faint light up ahead. He stopped short, causing Lief to walk into the back of him.

"—the hell?" Slurred the young man. "Why'd you stop?"

Rick squinted at the illumination, wondering if perhaps it was a side effect of some critical failure in his broken mind.

"You see that?" He said. "There's a light up there."

"—don't see shit," answered Lief. "You're crazy."

Rick moved forward again, pulling the rope taught and dragging his friend along with him.

"Hey! Where're we going?"

Gradually, as with the coming of the dawn, the light grew brighter and things crept into focus. The corridor was identical to so many they had explored already; filthy, damp, strewn with decay. The only difference now was that Rick could actually *see* it.

He hastened his pace, pupils constricting as the light continued to grow more dominant.

"What the hell, Rick?" Lief protested. "You're going too fast—I'm gonna trip."

Sound drifted down the corridor, vague at first, then clearer with each step. People were conversing, calling to one another as neighbors and friends. A blast of cool sea air swept across Rick's filthy face and a ship's bell tolled in the middle distance. Overcome with emotion, he broke into a run. The rope snapped taut and Leif was yanked off balance. Sprawling, the young man tangled himself in the line, which in turn caused Rick to lose his footing. A brief scramble ensued, Rick working to untie the knot at his waist, while Lief fumbled to find his flashlight.

Free of the snarl, Rick gained his footing once more and

staggered toward the end of the tunnel. Behind him, Lief's flashlight popped on, yet its glow was paltry in comparison to the ethereal light which now haloed the tunnel's mouth. Rick staggered into the light, moving through it, becoming part of it. When he emerged on the other side, he found himself standing amidst a scene that defied all notions of time and space.

People were everywhere, strolling arm-in-arm along a waterfront hung with impenetrable fog. Wearing herringbone jackets and coal-black top hats, the men nodded to one another, while their pale ladies flaunted corseted waistlines and pastel gowns. A carriage rattled past, drawn by four emaciated horses, their hooves flinging crimson blood. Drunken sailors and their painted harlots teetered in its wake, watched by native traders who stood smoking in the mud. Out of sight, yet wholly present, the shadows of familiar buildings lurked behind the veil of fog; silent and hulking.

Rick turned full circle, his legs as dizzy as his mind. The ship's bell tolled again and the fog swirled. Manifesting amidst the churn, the spray painter raised a hand in greeting. Clear in the light of the invisible sun, his face clung to his skull like an onion peel; discolored and wafer thin.

"You're almost there," he called to Rick. "He's waiting for you. They all are."

About to respond, Rick was interrupted by a roar of anger.

"Crazy son-of-a-bitch," shouted Lief, tackling him to the ground. "Trying to run away'n leave me down here?"

He seized Rick by the hair, scratching his face.

"I heard what you said! I know what you're planning!"

The flashlight arced, then streaked down, cracking against the side of Rick's head. Pain exploded in his right ear and warm blood seeped freely. Flickering, the invisible sun went out, taking with it the fog, the spray painter, the fancy people, and everything else that had existed in that fleeting snow globe of surreality. Darkness flooded in, leaving Rick with only one option; the hammer.

THE CITADEL OF THE
FORGOTTEN

Half limping, half stumbling through the darkness, Rick followed the sputtering orb of Lief's flashlight as it hurtled down yet another endless tunnel. Flecked with red, its glow painted a picture of madness and terror.

"G'away from me!" Screamed Lief. "You're crazy!"

The light swayed unsteadily, betraying the state of its wielder. Doubling his pace, Rick hefted the hammer; now sticky with blood. Lief vanished around the corner of a new tunnel, taking his light with him. Thrown into blindness, Rick fell upon his hands and knees and crawled like a spider. At the corner, he came upon something slumped against the wall and lashed out. The hammer scored the concrete with a shower of vanishing sparks. A mummified corpse flickered into existence; little more than dry bones and rotted cloth.

Lief screamed again, his panicked wails echoing throughout the catacombs. Rick left the mummy where it lay and continued on. The corridor shrank, becoming tighter and tighter until it was but a narrow aperture through which foul air rushed like the exhalations of a sulfurous pit.

Flattening himself, Rick contorted his body to the

breaking point, then bent some more. Something popped in his shoulder, and something tore in his knee. Claustrophobia reared its debilitating head, swallowing what little sanity he had left. Stuck fast, pressed between cold, immovable concrete, Rick succumbed to dread and fainted on the spot.

Vague sounds brought him back to consciousness, mechanical in nature; familiar even. Searching himself within, Rick found the wherewith all to force himself through the impossible passage until at last, he spilled out into a new corridor. Here, the mechanical sounds gained further clarity and a feeble illumination nipped at the edges of perception. Vomiting hot bile, Rick dragged a sleeve across his mouth and tried to stand up. His knee buckled with a crack, too weak to carry him. Forced to rely upon the wall for support, he slid along it like a shadow without a host.

The light grew brighter, then waned, then flared again, syncing with the rhythmic chugging of the machines. Far from gentle, it burned with an artificial incandescence that caused Rick to shield his eyes. He advanced at a shamble, allowing the gentle curve of the wall to guide him. When again he hazarded a glance, he had reached the end of the tunnel.

Rick stood recalcitrant, his unanchored mind drifting into deep waters. Lit by jaunty strings of carbide light bulbs, a secret city rose before him. Propped up with rusty I-beams and wreathed in acrid smoke, dozens of tessellated brickwork buildings leaned amidst the snarl of electric wires. Rick saw piles of rubble, and heaps of corroded mining equipment, and what seemed to be mounds of human waste, pouring from the narrow alleys. Continuing to dim and flare, the lights drew their inconsistent power from coal fire generators that hissed and chugged like ruptured engines of locomotion.

Gaping in disconcerted wonder, Rick waited for the spectral tolling of the ship's bell to bring about the impenetrable fog. Instead, a steam whistle blared its timeless call to work;

shrill and throaty. Movement stirred among the fetid hovels, outlines taking shape in the windows and doorways. Famine-thin and clad in tattered army outfits, a hoard of filthy creatures filed out into the street, pick-axes and shovels clutched in their withered hands. They marched in a body, making their way toward the further depths of the chamber, clambering over the mounds of their own stinking waste and human ruin.

The whistle died, and in its absence, Rick heard the miners chanting.

"Echto noctum para neisium. Echto noctum para neisium. Echto noctum para neisium. Baksha, Baksha, Baksha!"

HE WHO WAITS AT THE BOTTOM
OF THE ABYSS

Possessed by thoughts born of someone else's mind, Rick followed the chanting miners, deeper and deeper, limping along like a defective toy. Still clutched in his hand, the hammer swung back and forth; a metronome which kept time for the music of his madness.

The secret city drew to a pitiful end, its brick buildings crushed under the weight of their own impossibility. A train depot came next, filled with rotting cars that had long since rusted to the tracks. Piled high with rubble and mud, they tilted dangerously, while overhead, the lights dimmed. Rick saw the miners enter a new tunnel, framed by heavy metal blast doors. He shadowed their advance, leaving behind the incandescence of the depot for the dimly-lit shaft.

All at once, the concrete continuity of his prolonged imprisonment in the tunnels terminated, replaced by rough, bare rock. More mining equipment idled in the gloom, abandoned and overwrought with corrosion. Regressing from machine marks to those of hand tools, the walls told the story of a natural fissure, discovered and widened by curious Army engineers.

"Echto noctum para neisium," chanted the miners. *"Baksha, Baksha, Baksha!"*

Light flickered from the end of the tunnel, twisting with the elemental motion of fire. A small antechamber awaited, buttressed with rusty metal beams. At the far end, the mouth of a cavern took shape, splitting the rock like a lopsided smile. New sounds joined the chanting, those of pick-axes and grunting labor.

Rick limped forward, joining the miners as they queued before the opening. They paid him no mind, their faces as empty as they were unbearably gaunt. He saw Lief ahead of him, gripped by the same spell that compelled his own broken body to submit and follow. The boy glanced back, eyes framed by rivulets of dried blood.

The lopsided smile opened to consume them, revealing a cavern so enormous and infinite that it perverted all notions of possibility. Rick keeled beneath the ocean of blackness, while distantly, the chanting grew more fervent.

"Echto noctum para neisium. Baksha, Baksha, Baksha!"

Torches burned in rows, yet even their presence did nothing to unmask the true size and scope of the cavern. Grouped in a wide circle, they rimmed the edge of a yawning quarry, carved into the very bedrock of the immortal earth itself. Men climbed up from the depths, their daily toil having ended at the arrival of the next shift. Rick watched them go, filthy and on the verge of utter collapse. It seemed that they had been at their work for decades, centuries even, sustained by the eating of their own dead and theft of countless lost children.

The pit called to him, its contents demanding witness. He staggered to the rim, finding Lief similarly compelled. The two men stared down into the sooty darkness, where haphazard scaffolding had been constructed to further the excavation of a truth too terrible to comprehend. Laying on its back in funeral respite, a colossal skeleton filled the

28

bottom of the pit like a fallen tower of bones. Rick blinked, then blinked again, his eyes tracing vertebrae the size of semi trucks, and a rib cage large enough to house an entire battleship. He saw boney hands with fingers as long as fallen trees, and a skull whose sockets were so craterous that they could drink the mind of every man, woman, and child on the planet.

Lief began to scream, and as he did so, the miners stopped their chanting.

"Surface men," they said in a single voice. *"Know you now the origin of death."*

Glowing from within, coming to life despite its obvious fossilization, the giant skeleton at the bottom of the pit turned its unthinkable awareness on Rick and Lief. Already but a remnant of a thing once whole, Rick's mind blew apart in a kaleidoscopic paroxysm of incomprehensible truth. He rocketed up through the layers of his consciousness, bursting through them like a mortar round launched at the pitted surface of the living moon. Patterns of light and sound filled the vacuum, and streamers of auroral brilliance painted the inside of his eyelids. Distantly, with what little sense remained, he became aware that Lief was not with him on his rocketing trajectory. Too fragile to make the journey, the boy had fallen to the bottom of the pit, dashed to bits upon the domed skull of the long-dead Titan.

The Maintenance Man

When Rick awoke, he was laying upon the beach in a shivering heap. Seawater sucked at his ankles, threatening to draw him along with the outgoing tide where fish and crabs would make a scant meal of his drowned corpse. He clambered up in the predawn gloom and lurched, failingly, toward the lighthouse at Point Wilson. Crashing up through the beachgrass, he gained the parking lot where several tourists had already gathered to watch the rising sun. Their backs were turned to him, their minds tainted with contagious ignorance.

Rick reached out with hands caked in blood, gore, and other less recognizable filth. And yet, before he could attack, a police cruiser screeched into the parking lot and a pair of officers leaped out from within. They tackled Rick savagely, slamming his bloody head against the concrete and cuffing his hands.

Though he no longer had a voice to call his own, he screamed at them in wild protest.

"You can't do this!"

"Baksha!"

"You have to listen to me!"

"Baksha! Baksha!"

"I'm from here!"

"Baksha!"

"It's still happening!"

Made in the USA
Middletown, DE
14 August 2023

36618874R00021